Wally The Watermelon's Wild And Whacky Weekday Walks

EILEEN DISTASIO-CLARK

With Great Love and Appreciation to Those Who Have and Do Bless My Life.

My Family:

Joseph DeStasio Sr. & Miriam Lucille Baragone DeStasio, My Late Parents.

Andrea Jean DeStasio McIntosh, My Older Sister and Their Families.

Joseph DeStasio Jr., My Younger and Only Brother and Their Families.

Donna Marie DeStasio Wagner, My Younger Sister and Their Families.

My Children:

Eileen, Rebekah, Rachel, S. Michael,

Jennifer, Sharon, Tara, Stephanie,

Apryll, Mikaelah, & M. Trevor

and THEIR Families!!

ACKNOWLEDGMENTS

First and foremost, I express, deeply, my sincere gratitude to our Heavenly Father for blessing me with the gift and talent of writing! I know I could not do what I do without His assistance.

I also want to acknowledge and express gratitude to my children, Eileen, Rebekah, Rachel, S. Michael, Jennifer, Sharon, Tara, Stephanie, Apryll, Mikaelah, and M. Trevor, who were very active in 'creating' many tales about the Hunk-a-Doodles.

Truth be told, I really do not know how we came up with the name, Hunk-a-Doodles, but I give the credit for that to my children. I must also credit them for the inspirations that produced these stories because it was through their sweet and innocent childhood antics that they were originally originated!

INTRODUCTION

In 1992, shortly after my family moved to Missouri, I found, in a Clearance Sale Bin in the Hy-Vee grocery store, five stuffed fruits: a cherry, a lemon, an orange, a plum, and a watermelon. They were so cute I just had to buy them!

Once home, I put them on the half wall that separated the kitchen from the living room, where they sat for the whole time that we lived in that house. Now, of course, any time we had to move, they did too. We loved them too much to leave them behind!

In different homes, they usually sat in different places, on the wall above the stairs, on a bed, usually mine, on the back of the couch, on... well, just wherever we wanted them to sit. But sitting was not all that they did.

We played with them, we used them to decorate for special occasions, we... well, we just had a great deal of fun with them!

We called them our Hunk-a-Doodles, but I really do not recall how we came up with that name. We also gave each one of them their own name. The cherry was identified as Chad, the orange was named Ollie, the lemon was called Larry, the plum was Peter, and the watermelon was given the name Wally!

We also made up fun stories with them and that is what motivated me to write these stories to share with you! So, please read and enjoy them, over and over and over again!

WALLY THE WATERMELON'S WILD AND WHACKY WEEKDAY WALKS

It was a quiet Monday morning,

The summer sun lit up the sky!

And Wally, who was an early riser,

To the sleeping Hunks, said, "Bye, bye!"

Wally was taking his morning walk,

He did that every day.

And on most mornings, he left quite early,

Before breakfast, which was the real start of the day!

So, quietly he walked,

Down the hall and down the stairs,

Then stepped out on the porch,

And walked around the chairs!

Off the porch, he lightly did spring,

And scampered down the path.

He skipped and hopped, jumped and ran,

To the lake they called a bath!

*****Side Note:** The lake was really called Lake Bass, but Haleakim, who was another one of the Hunks' very best friends, renamed it for herself. Well for herself and for all the Hunk-a-Doodles, which by the way, I am certain you know, are Chad the Cherry, Ollie the Orange, Larry the Lemon, Peter the Plum, and Wally the Watermelon. Anyway, the reason Haleakim decided she wanted to call it Lake Bath was because the water was so warm that when she swam in the lake, she felt like she was taking a bath.

Okay, now that I explained that and I hope it makes sense to you, we can hop back to the other side.***

"Wow," Wally said as he walked down Primary Path.

"It is such a nice morning, so warm and quiet,

"And the breeze is swaying the trees.

"I want to climb one; maybe I should try it."

"But I guess I really do not know,

"If that would be smart to do.

"Haleakim said that is only good,

"If someone else is with you."

"So, I guess I will not do that now.

"I will just walk... oh wow!

"What is that? Let me see.

"I wonder what that could be."

***Uh, Another **Side Note:** Every time Wally took a walk, and I do mean every time, he always found something. Now, that may seem rather odd to some people, but not to Wally. He knew the people who lived in the Land of Never-Could-Happen very well. And he knew that for them, what 'never could happen' always happened, and losing things seemed to be one of those things. So, for Wally, one his motivations for his early morning walks, though it was not the only one; Wally truly did love to take walks. Anyway, one of the reasons he loved those walks so much was because he always, and I do mean every day, found something. And, since, to him, they were treasures, that was one of the things he loved best about his walks.

Now, let us go back to the other side so we can see what it was that Wally saw.***

As Wally made a right turn off Primary Path onto Sunbeam Street, he saw a tiny bit of something sticking out from under a pile of sticks. It looked like a... well maybe a... well, actually, Wally could not see what it looked like. So, he decided to climb over the fence that was between him and Sandyman Park, which is where the pile of sticks was piled, and go see for himself what it was he was seeing, or not really seeing.

He climbed up the fence just fine, but once at the top, instead of just climbing down the other side, and probably because the fence was not that high, probably only about 4' high, he decided to jump. And when he did... well, he did not land well. You see, it was not his feet that hit the ground; it was his bottom. And, being so round, when he hit the ground, he rolled and rolled and ro... well, I am certain you know what he did. When he finally stopped rolling, just a few feet from the pile of sticks, he got up and hopped like a bunny rabbit to the pile.

Now, to be able to pull from under the sticks pile, the thing that he saw, he pulled a few of the sticks that were directly on top of—whatever it was—and then, as the whole pile fell down, he said to himself:

"Oh, Wally! Now, look what you did.

"Whatever it was, you now fully hid.

"I guess, all these sticks, I will have to rid,

"So, I can see what it was that was hid."

And that was exactly what he did. He restacked the sticks, which did not take very long because there were really not many sticks. Then he turned back to where the pile had first been, and when he saw what had been hidden, he said:

"Wowzers Trowzers! What is this?

"And what are those two things I did miss?

"They look like tools I have never seen.

"I wonder how long—here—they have been!"

Then, picking up the first tool, which was a wrench, he said to himself:

"Hmm, this looks cool! It is a tool!"

Picking up the second tool, which was a measuring tape, he added:

"It is used as a tool... er; well, it measures as a ruler."

But when he picked up the third tool, which…, well this is what he said:

"Hmm… I think I should not call this a tool,

"If I did, myself, I might fool.

"I know it really is not, you see.

"It is just a Ball-Tie Bungee.

Then as Wally put them into the sack that he always took with him on his walks, he wondered:

'How are these used and why are they here? I really would like to know.

'I wonder who left them, or lost them or… Well, I wonder to whom they should go.'

Since Sandyman Park had some pretty nice trails, Wally decided that would be where he did his Monday walk. So, he scampered from tree to tree down all the trails, which were connected to each other, running around every tree he came to, and then, when he got to the end of the last trail, he decided to run across the park to the fence where he had entered the park. But, when he started running through the picnic pavilion, he quickly stopped because he saw something on the ground right in front of the fireplace. So, he changed his direction and skipped over to the fireplace. There on the ground were three drink bottles: a purple one with stickers on it, a red one, a green one, a small blue cup—of some sort, and a baby-sized fork with a red handle. Of course, he picked those up too, put them in his sack, and then continued his walk home, which was really not a walk because across the rest of Sandyman Park, over the fence, down Sunbeam Street and Primary Path, Wally skipped, jumped, ran, and even rolled.

Side Note Number Two:** Question for you! Are you beginning to see why I call Wally's walks wild and whacky? I think you might be. But read on; I am certain you will see even better as you do. Now, back to the other side.

Once home, seeing that Chad, Ollie, Larry, and Peter were all awake and ready for the day, he enthusiastically showed them what he had found. While they were all rather impressed. After all, among all the things Wally had ever found, tools, drink bottles, a strange cup, and a baby fork had never been among them.

Therefore, Chad said, "I wonder who lost them."

And Ollie added, "I do too."

Then Larry replied, "Yes, good question."

And Peter suggested, "Well, we know what we must do."

So, Wally ventured:

"Yep, so with the rest of this week's finds, and we all know there will be more,

"This will be the first in the "Found-You-Box" we store.

"Then on Sunday, as we always do,

"We will try to find whom these belong to."

Then, in unison, they all 'sang' together:

"But right now, it is breakfast time, so let each of us take a seat,

"And all sit down at the table, our yummy pancake breakfast to eat."

And that was exactly what they did!

Now, as you probably already figured out, every day began the same way. So, I will just tell you about Wally's walks and that way, we can move more quickly to Sunday.

Tuesday, Wally took his walk through Friendly Farm Park.

'Friendly Farm Park?' You are probably questioning, 'Was it a farm or was it a park?'

Well, I will answer that question for you; it was both! You see, Mr. Challim and his wife, Hanncy, owned a pretty nice farm. But actually, it was a ranch because, instead of growing food crops, they raised, boarded, and trained horses. Now, of course, they did also have their own garden, where they grew food for themselves, and which they shared with others. So, because they raised, boarded, and trained horses and grew some food, they called their place a Frarmanch.

'What?' You are now asking, 'What is a Frarmanch?'

Well, I can explain that to you too. Since they did grow some food, it was a farm. And, since they raised, boarded, and trained horses, it was also a ranch. So, they separated the F from the ARM in the word farm, and the R from the ANCH in the word ranch. Then they put those letters together in their own order, and came up with FRARMANCH!

Now, just as soon as you can stop laughing, I will finish to answer your question.

Okay, it sounds like you are now done laughing, so I will continue.

Because they are such nice, friendly, generous people, as are pretty much all of the people in both the Land of Never-Could-Happen and the Valley of Down-Below, they wanted to share their blessings with whomever they could. So, they put up a fence around a pretty nice-sized part of their Frarmanch and placed some picnic tables there. That way, anyone who wanted to, could spend some relaxing time in their park, which they had named Friendly Farm Park.

Now that you understand all of that, let us get back to Wally's Tuesday Walk.

Wally loved the Challims and he loved their park, so on Tuesday, he had decided to walk to Friendly Farm Park and eat his breakfast there. And that day, Chad, Ollie, Larry, Peter and Haleakim went with him because they all loved the Challim's park too.

When they got to the park, they sat down at the table closest to the fence on the farm side of the park because they wanted to watch the horses eat their breakfast, AKA graze in the pastures, while they—the Hunks and Haleakim—ate their breakfasts, which were nuts, berries, and ice-cold water!

Chad, not being an early riser, was still a little bit tired, so he just sat quietly and watched the horses, while he ate his cranberries and almonds.

Ollie, who also was not an early riser, sat quietly too, almost falling asleep, while he ate his blueberries and pecans as he watched the birds fly around the horses.

Larry, who was unusually peppy and not typically being an early riser either, ate his blackberries and walnuts as he watched the horses graze on the grass.

Peter, who sometimes was, and sometimes was not, an early riser, watched the horses and the squirrels, as he ate his raspberries and hazelnuts.

Wally, whom you already know was an early riser, had a hard time sitting still as he watched the horses, birds, and squirrels, while he ate his strawberries and chestnuts.

And Haleakim, who was another early riser, sang with the birds as she bounced up and down, as if she were on the back of a horse. While she watched them eat their breakfast, as she ate hers, which was a combination of cranberries, blueberries, blackberries, raspberries, and strawberries mixed with almonds, pecans, walnuts, hazelnuts, and chestnuts.

When they were all done eating, they cleaned off the table, tossed the trash into the bin that was aside from the table, and began walking around the park, all the while watching the horses, the birds, the squirrels, and any other animals that came into view.

But what captured Wally's attention the most were the two hats, the shower slides, and the little kid's shoes that he had found at the bottom of a tree on the far side of the park.

"Oh, figgle-dee-wiggle-dee," Wally said. "Look what I just found.

"Whoever would have thought you could find this stuff on the ground."

Now, you could possibly be wondering why the other Hunks did not find what Wally had found, since they were all walking together. Well, that explanation is simple. While Chad, Ollie, Larry, and Peter were actually walking, Wally was not; he was crawling! Yes! You read that right; he was crawling on the ground, around the trees and the trash cans, over the rocks and the tree stumps, and around and under the tables. And it was when he had crawled out from under one of the tables that he saw the hats: one black and the other green and white, a black pair of little girl's shoes with white polka-dotted bows, and a black pair of shower sliders with white strips across the top.

After the other Hunks and Haleakim sat down on the ground next to Wally to see what he had found. They were rather stunned. Well, all except Haleakim. So, Haleakim explained this to them. He said, "People do not always keep their hats and shoes on. Maybe some people do, but most do not. So, sometimes, especially if they are having a get-together with others, thinking that someone else packed up all the stuff when it was time to go, things get left behind."

"Oh," the Hunks replied. "We see, we really do, but it does make us sad, we feel boohoo!"

"You really do not have to feel boo-hoo," Haleakim said. "You can just put them in your Found-You-Box and take them to church on Sunday."

Now the made them all feel better, so they got up. Wally put the shoes and hats in his bag, and they continued their walk around the rest of the park before returning home.

On Wednesday morning, when Chad, Ollie, Larry, and Peter were getting breakfast ready, Wally bounded into the house with extra highly heightened emotion.

"Hey Guys!" Wally shouted as he bounded through the door.

"Come look! Come look! Come look!" he said, as he spread his finds out on the floor.

"I found a bunch of things today as I walked down Merry Miss Lane.

"Some of them were just on the ground, but some were in the drain."

As his buddies sat down on the floor in front of him, Wally spread out the things that he had found, and then, as he pointed to each one, he said:

"When I started down the lane, I tripped over these."

He paused to hold up a car key fob with four keys.

"I fell down on the ground, landing on this."

Pausing again, he held up a key that he almost did miss.

"Then I rolled down the hill to Comfort Court,

"And stopping, with my face to the ground,

"I saw two things of a different sort,

"A lanyard with a key and bracelet, wiggly round."

"I picked them up, and myself to, then walked across the street.

"And carefully stepped onto the curb,

"But when I looked down, I saw something by my feet.

"It was this lanyard that I thought smelt like an herb."

"When I looked between the bars, to my joy,

"I saw something in there too.

"It was this little plastic monkey toy,

"And there were sunglasses that were blue."

"That was when Haleakim happened to come by,

"And I asked her for some help, after we said 'Hi.'

"So, with a stick, poking through the bars,

"She was able to pull them up and now they are ours."

"Then on my way home, I found a glasses case,

"Black with white polka dots, and two more glasses for the face.

"Pink and black they were under the bushes that I was crawling though,

"And with them pacifiers, one white and one blue."

Now, of course, Chad, Ollie, Larry, and Peter were all very impressed. While it was very usual for Wally to find things when he took his walks, he did not usually find that much stuff on just one walk. Then after helping Wally clean all the stuff, he found, they also helped him put it in the Found-You-Box.

On Thursday, Wally took his walk on the Targeteer Trail, and Haleakim went with him. Being as curious as he is, when Wally saw a hole in the trunk of a tree they were passing, he naturally had to stop, hop over to the tree, and look into the hole. And when he did, he cried out with excitement:

"A shark! A shark! Little and blue, I think I will really like you!"

"A shark?" Haleakim questioned, then also asked, "Wally, what are you looking at?"

Wally reached into the hole in the tree trunk, as far as he could, but having such small arms, he could not reach the shark. Seeing what the problem was, Haleakim said, "Here, Wally, let me get it out for you." Then she put her hand into the hole in the tree trunk, felt something soft and plushy, grabbed it, and pulled it out. Indeed, it was a small, blue, soft, plushy toy in the image of a shark, with a blue clasp attached to its back.

"Oh, this is really cute," Haleakim said, as she handed it to Wally. "You can put this in your Found-You-Box, too. I bet when you take this to church on Sunday, you will find the person who lost it. At least I hope you do. I think whoever lost it must be very sad to not have it."

As Wally looked at the pretty blue shark and felt is softness, he replied to Haleakim:

"Yes, yes indeed, to church with me, it must go,

"For super sad its owner must be, that I surely do know!"

Wally dropped the shark into his bag as they crossed over Crystal Creek Bridge. Skipping and hopping they made their way to the end of Targeteer Trail, and then headed back to the Hunk's home, going through the Peaceful Playground. As they passed the big swing set, Ollie found three more stuffed animals: a crazy-looking grey, blue, red, and orange duck, a whiteish pig wearing a red dress and holding a... well, whatever she was holding, and a grey quokka with a black nose, brown feet, and tan hands. Of course, he picked them all up and stuffed them in his bag with the shark. Once home, after saying bye-bye to Haleakim, he went inside, showed his finds to Chad, Ollie, Larry, and Peter, and then, after they all played with them for a little while, he put all four stuffed animals into the Found-You-Box.

On Friday, Wally's Walk was through the Believe-It-Or-Not Ball Park, and yes, he found balls, a lot of balls—thirteen balls—and, oh yes, he even found a golf ball tee. Now, truth be told, it was not the easiest of his finds. You see, Wally had a way of... hmm... should I say 'dropping himself' just about everywhere. And that was what he did in the ballpark. He just kept falling down. And every time he fell down, he found another ball.

Now, you may be wondering why he fell down so much. Well, just in case you are wondering, I will tell you. Wally was not watching where he was going; he was looking up at and reading all the billboards that surrounded the park. So, he did not see the balls until he had stepped on them and fallen down. Now, of course, it goes without saying, he also picked up the balls and took them home.

'What kind of balls were they?' You are probably wondering.

So, I will tell you what they were. There were seven tennis balls, two golf balls, one plastic toy baseball, one squishy ball, one teeny tiny game ball, and one red, white, yellow, blue, pink, and green blow-up plastic water ball. Oh, and the golf tee was blue.

Then on Saturday, his last walk of that week, Wally strolled down Best Boulevard, where he found three bracelets: one red, one white, one blue, and one gold; and a mini flag that had written on it 'Just Married.' Then, as he strolled back up Best Boulevard, he found a framed drawing of a pretty pink rose.

Well, needless to say, but I will say it anyway, all the Hunks loved all the stuff that Wally had found, and they loved it so much that they were more tempted than they had ever been to just keep it all. But they knew that that was not, and would never be, the right thing to do unless it was completely impossible for them to find out to whom it had belonged and return it to them, if they wanted it. So, on Sunday…

With the bag that held all forty-eight things that Wally had found that week, the Hunks walked to church. On the way there, and once there, both before began, and after it ended, they asked everyone they met and everyone who was at church if any of the stuff was theirs. Now, while most of the Lone Descendants of Santo told them, "No, I did not lose anything," there were a few who did and they were so very grateful that, not only had the Hunks found it, but they were returning it.

Eneile was very grateful that the Hunks had found her daddy's tools. He had been pretty upset with himself for losing them. So grateful was she that, after receiving the wrench and measuring tape, she told them they could keep the bungee cord.

The keys, lanyards, wallet, and glasses cases were claimed by HaKeber, whose children had lost them when they had been out taking a walk with their friends. They had gone to so many different places that they really had no idea where to go to look for the stuff they had lost. They, too, were so grateful to the Hunks that they gave them the wallet as their way to say thanks!

The Hunks also had found the true owners of the hats and shoes, Norash and Rata, who were equally as grateful as the others to have their things back again. They let the Hunks keep the green and white hat.

Now, while the Hunks were so very happy that they had been able to find the owners of some of the stuff, they really wanted to see if they could find the owners of the rest of the stuff too. So, they spent the rest of the day, visiting people all over the Land of Never-Could-Happen and the Valley of Down-Below. And their efforts did pay off because, by the end of the day, they had been able to return the sunglasses, pacifiers, and little plastic monkey to ReFinjen's family, the drink bottles, little blue cup and the baby fork to Einahpets' sisters, and all the balls to LeAchim and Rovert. But that was all.

So, they left, on the doorstep of LeChar's house, the three little bracelets; on the doorstep of Lalpry's house, the stuffed shark and pig; on the doorstep of Haleakim's house, the stuffed duck; and at the Good Deed for the Day Donation Center the 'Just Married' flag.

Finally, they went home, cleaned the bungee cord, the wallet, the green and white hat, the stuffed quokka, and the beautiful picture of the pink rose as best they could, attached this note to the picture of the rose, and they placed them in their glass Special Treasures display case:

Happiness, Purity, and Gratitude are traits these roses project.

Gentleness and selflessness are what they let us expect!

So, we will always do what we can to help others feel their best,

And this is a promise, solemn, not just words of jest!

The End...

Or is it the,

Another Step?

ABOUT THE AUTHOR

Eileen DiStasio-Clark is the second oldest of four children. She is the mother of eleven children and grandmother to twenty-three grandchildren, to date. As a member of The Church of Jesus Christ of Latter-Day Saints, she serves in various positions, teaching, leading, and ministering to children, youth, and adults. Currently, she is also a Family History Missionary. Eileen established the Pursuit of Excellence Institute of Family Education, a non-profit organization focused on strengthening the family. Presently she holds an A.A., a B.A., and an M.A. in Clinical Psychology and is working on the completion of her Doctoral Degree.